The Lima Bear™ Stories

HOW BACK-BACK GOT HIS NAME

Story By Charles A. Neebe
Illustrations By Len DiSalvo

Lima Bear Press, LLC
PO Box 354
Montchanin, DE 19710-0354
Phone/fax is: 302-691-4799
email: lbp.books@yahoo.com   website: www.limabearpress.com

Kiwanis International

"Books for Kids"

Success through reading

A Detroit www.kiwanis1.org Service Project

Book design by: Len DiSalvo and George Clements
Cover design by: Len DiSalvo and George Clements
ISBN: 1 - 933872 - 20 -9

Library of Congress Control Number: 2006935080

Printed in China
Published by Lima Bear Press
PO Box 354, Montchanin, DE 19710-0354
Bulk Orders: lbp.books@yahoo.com

The Lima Bear™ Stories

How Back-Back Got His Name

Story By Charles A. Neebe
Illustrations By Len DiSalvo

One cool autumn morning, Lima Bear lay sleeping in his walnut-shell bed inside a small abandoned hollow in the Big Oak tree. He looked a bit like a lima bean with his round green belly, short arms and legs all snuggled up in his tiny bed.

Suddenly, there was a loud call from outside!

"Wake-up, Lima Bear! Wake UP!!!"

"Oh my!" the startled Lima Bear exclaimed as he popped straight into the air and landed on his stubby legs and rushed out.

"What, Whistle-Toe?"

"Lima Bear, we have an EEE-mergency!!!"

The rabbit held a note out for Lima Bear to read. It said:

I HAVE AN EEE-MERGENCY.
PLUMPTON

Without a word, Lima Bear climbed onto Whistle-Toe's back and, holding onto his fur, they rushed off to their friend, Plumpton, the Opossum.

Inside Plumpton's hole in the ground, Whistle-Toe hopped excitedly as they waited to hear about the EEE-mergency.

"Do you see anything different about me?" Plumpton asked sadly.

"Well," Whistle-Toe said, "you look plump and hairy, but that's nothing new."

"I've lost something very important. I've lost my... my back." Plumpton's eyes filled with tears.

"Your back?!" Whistle-Toe said almost stopping in mid-air.

"Your back? I don't understand," Lima Bear said. Facing Whistle-Toe and Lima Bear, Plumpton slowly turned around and, as he turned, he DISAPPEARED! Where his back should have been, there was nothing.

"Aaaaaa-MAAY-zing!" Whistle-Toe exclaimed, "Do that again!"

"This is serious," Lima Bear said. "How did this happen?"

"I don't know. When I was brushing my fur this morning, I looked in the mirror and saw my back was...was GONE!" Plumpton turned to face his friends and became visible once again. "Who ever heard of an animal without a back? Everyone in the forest will laugh at me! Oh, what am I to do?"

"Don't worry, Plumpton, we'll help you find your back," Lima Bear said. "Hmmm...., but we'll need all the help we can get. Let's find Maskamal, too."

Maskamal, the raccoon, frowned with concentration. "Turn around again, Plumpton."

Plumpton turned around and disappeared and then reappeared. Maskamal scratched his head. Suddenly, his face lit up. "I know."

"How to find my back?"

"No, of course not. Look, this is not a usual EEE-mergency, so we need a different way of thinking."

"What?" Whistle-Toe asked, puzzled. "I only know how to think the way a rabbit thinks."

"Same with me," Plumpton said. "I only think like an opossum."

"Ah-ha, a clue," Lima Bear said. "Since it's your back that's missing, we all need to think the way an opossum thinks. That would be a different way of thinking, at least for the rest of us. Plumpton, how does an opossum think?"

"I don't know. I only know that we do our best thinking hanging upside down."

"There, you see," Lima Bear said, "that's what we need to do."

Plumpton led them to his favorite tree. "There's my branch---best one for thinking." They looked up, way up, until they saw where Plumpton was pointing. Maskamal's eyes widened.

"You mean... all the way up there?"

"Well, yes," Plumpton said.

"I'll stay down here," Whistle-Toe said, "just in case some of us think better on the ground."

Lima Bear hung on to Maskamal. With Plumpton gently pushing them from underneath, they slowly climbed up the trunk of the tree. If the branch had looked high from were they were standing on the ground, now it seemed higher still. When they arrived, Plumpton nudged Maskamal and Lima Bear out onto the branch and wrapped Maskamal's tail around it. Looking down, Maskamal felt dizzy. "Help! I'm fallllling," he yelled as he fell off.

"Well done, Maskamal," Plumpton said. "You did that just like an opossum."

Maskamal was swinging by his tail. He was so frightened he couldn't speak. Plumpton turned to Lima Bear. He realized Lima Bear's tail was not nearly long enough. "Oh well, at least Maskamal's doing it right. He can try the different way of thinking for all of us."

"Help!" Maskamal yelled, at last able to speak.

"Maskamal, are you thinking like an opossum?" Plumpton asked hopefully.

"Save me!"

"Oh, dear," Lima Bear said. "I'm afraid this isn't working so well."

The two tried to pull Maskamal up, but he was too heavy.

"Now we have a second EEE-mergency," Lima Bear said. "Hold on Maskamal. We'll think of something." He looked down below for Whistle-Toe, but Whistle-Toe had grown tired of waiting and had taken off in search of Plumpton's back by himself. "Maybe if we climb down we can figure out how to reach Maskamal from the ground," Plumpton said.

"Don't leave me!" Maskamal cried.

"Don't worry, Maskamal," Lima Bear said. "I'll stay here with you."

Plumpton climbed down the tree. He reached up, but Maskamal was hanging way above him. "If only I could make myself taller," Plumpton thought.

Plumpton looked around, but all he saw were thousands of red, yellow and brown leaves that had fallen onto the ground. That was it! A pile of leaves! He would make a huge pile of leaves and stand on them to reach Maskamal.

He began pushing the leaves into a big pile. But every time he stood on the pile, he just sank down as if he were on a pillow.

"Quick," he thought, "I must make the pile bigger."

Meanwhile, Lima Bear had climbed to a higher branch to try to see where Whistle-Toe had gone. Stretching as tall as he could, he spotted Whistle-Toe at the far end of Big Meadow, hopping frantically about, trapped inside a cage! The shock of seeing his friend trapped made Lima Bear lose his balance, and he fell, smack onto Maskamal's tail.

The surprise made Maskamal lose his grip, and the two of them tumbled down into Plumpton's pile of leaves.

Brushing the leaves off, Lima Bear said: "Plumpton, that was so clever."

"It was?" Plumpton asked. "What was?"

"Building that pile of leaves."

"Oh," Plumpton said, not understanding.

"Making a soft place for us to land. Plumpton, you're a hero."

"Oh," Plumpton said. Then, suddenly beaming he added: "Yes, that was clever, wasn't it."

"But now," Lima Bear said urgently, "we have another EEE-mergency! Whistle-Toe's been captured. He's in a cage at the end of Big Meadow. We must save him!"

They came to the edge of Big Meadow and, at the far side, saw Whistle-Toe inside a cage. The boys and girls who had captured him were playing in the meadow.

"We must rescue him," Maskamal said.

"I'll try," Lima Bear said. "I'm small enough that no one will see me."

Brave Lima Bear started out. For him, it was like a jungle. He had to climb over the blades of grass. As he neared the middle, suddenly there was a 'whooosh' as a big round object rolled past him. He did not know it was a soccer ball. He thought it was a large round stone. Then, there was the pounding of feet and shouting as the children rushed past, chasing the big round stone. Their feet landed all around Lima Bear nearly stepping on him. Just as he was catching his breath, there was another 'whooosh' as the big round stone rolled past in the other direction followed by the pounding feet. Lima Bear hid under a leaf.

He hurried as fast as he could to escape from this terrible big round stone. Suddenly, 'kaplunk', something landed on Lima Bear and pinned him to the ground. Everything went dark. The soccer ball had landed right on top of him. "Oh, now they've caught me, too." Lima Bear cried.

Then, 'boom', the ball was kicked into the air. Lima Bear was free. The big feet pounded past him, and he rushed to Whistle-Toe.

"Oh, Lima Bear, thank goodness," Whistle-Toe said. "I don't want to live in a cage."

The cage was fastened with wooden pegs. Lima Bear tried to push one peg out, but it would not move. He found a small pebble and, using it as a hammer, he tried to pound the peg out, but he wasn't big enough. "Don't worry, Whistle-Toe," he said. "We won't leave you here."

Lima Bear started across the meadow, but the big round stone was chasing him so much that he had to keep changing direction to escape it. With all this changing of direction, he became lost. When Lima Bear did not return, the other two thought he had been captured, too - another EEE-mergency.

"I'll try," Maskamal said. "But first I'll need a disguise." And so while Plumpton kept watch, Maskamal went off. He needed a clever disguise. His eyes lit up.

A tree! He would disguise himself as a tree. Maskamal found a big, wet mud-hole. He jumped into it and rolled around until he was dripping with mud. Then he rolled in the pile of leaves that Plumpton had made. His whole body was covered with stuck leaves. He looked filthy. "Perfect," he thought to himself. "This will fool everybody. The children will never recognize me." Just to be extra certain, he found two dead branches and held them out, one in each arm.

Plumpton did not hear Maskamal returning. Maskamal stood behind him. "This is going to be fun," he thought. "I'll call out and then let's see him try to find me." He held out his two branches. "Pssst. Hey, Plumpton, look."

"Oh, dear," Plumpton said. "Maskamal, you had an accident."

"Don't be silly. This is my disguise."

"Your disguise? Being dirty isn't much of a disguise."

"No, no!" Maskamal said. "Come on, think. What's the disguise?"

"I don't know. Well,..... maybe."

"What?"

"A... a raccoon-with-leaves disguise?"

"No!" Maskamal said. "A tree! What's the matter with you? You have no imagination. This'll fool those children."

"But Maskamal, there're no trees in Big Meadow."

"Details, details," Maskamal said. "I'm going to rescue Whistle-Toe. That's all that counts." Maskamal started out.

The boys and girls were playing soccer at the far end of the Big Meadow and did not notice him. Slowly, Maskamal moved toward them. "It's working," he said to himself.

Then one of the boys yelled: "Look, guys, a raccoon. Let's get him." The children all stopped playing and started running toward Maskamal. Now Maskamal was sure that the children were talking about some other raccoon. They could not possibly have seen through his disguise. Maskamal smiled and held out his arms as far as he could and tried even harder to look like a tree. Strangely, though, the children seemed to be coming right toward him.

"That other raccoon must be right behind me," Maskamal thought. "I wish he'd go away. He's spoiling everything." The children were almost upon Maskamal now and yelling: "Grab him. Look how dirty he is."

"How dirty he is?? Hey, that's me!" Maskamal thought. 'Thud'. He dropped the branches and ran for his life, the leaves flying off him. But it was too late. They caught him, and now he was in a cage, too.

Oh, my-my," Plumpton said. "Now we have another EEE-mergency. And Lima Bear's gone too. It's all my fault. I'll have to give it a try. But I'm so afraid."

Plumpton started out across Big Meadow. He was so frightened that he could hardly breathe. Whenever the children turned even a little in his direction, he lay down and played dead - what an opossum always does when in danger. He was so afraid that little did he realize that, when he lay on his stomach, he became completely invisible.

Meanwhile, Lima Bear at last found his way back. Climbing up on a small twig, he saw Plumpton making his way across Big Meadow, laying down many times, each time completely disappearing. "Plumpton is SO clever," Lima Bear thought.

Plumpton pulled out the pegs and he and Whistle-Toe and Maskamal escaped before the boys and girls knew what had happened. They raced back to their staring point and, with joy, found Lima Bear safe and sound. With Lima Bear clinging to Maskamal, the four friends returned to Plumpton's house.

"It is a good thing we didn't find your back after all," Lima Bear said.

"Why?" Plumpton asked.

"Because you were so smart. You made yourself invisible to those children."

"I did?"

"You know" Lima Bear said, "whenever you lay down."

"You mean when I was playing dead?"

"Yes, every time you did that, you made yourself invisible."

"Oh." Plumpton thought for a few moments. Then a proud look spread across his face. "Yes, that was rather smart, wasn't it?"

"Our rescuer!" Whistle-Toe and Maskamal said together.

"You know," Plumpton said, "maybe being different isn't so bad."

"You can do special things because you're different," Lima Bear said. "And, to think, all this time we were trying to get your back back"

"Wait," Whistle-Toe said. "I like that name."

"What name?" Plumpton asked.

"Back-Back. We should call you Back-Back."

"But I already have a name," Plumpton said.

"I know," Whistle-Toe said, "but Back-Back is a name for someone who can do special things."

"Yes," Lima Bear said. "That's a great name. Back-Back – two times a hero."

Plumpton, or rather Back-Back, smiled. "It is a rather nice name."

"Done then," Lima Bear declared.

And that's how Back-Back got his name.

12
120
/240